WHERE IS THAT CAT?

CAROL GREENE
ILLUSTRATED BY LORETTA KRUPINSKI

HYPERION BOOKS FOR CHILDREN

NEW YORK

Library of Congress Cataloging-in-Publication Data
Greene, Carol.
Where is that cat? / Carol Greene ; illustrated by Loretta Krupinski
p. cm.
Summary : While trying to give away the cat she has found, Miss Perkins
gradually grows fond enough of him that she decides to keep him.
ISBN 0-7868-0457-2 (trade)— ISBN 0-7868-2399-2 (library)
PZ7.G82845No   1998   [E]—dc21   98-11586

One snowy day, Miss Perkins went out to get her mail. She found one letter, two bills, and a cat.

"Hello, cat," she said. "What's your name?"

Just then a snowflake landed on the cat's nose.
"Fitz!" he sneezed.

"Fitz," said Miss Perkins. "That's a good name.
Well, you'd better come in, Fitz. It's too cold out
here for you."

She took him into the kitchen and gave him some tuna and a bowl of milk.

"Now, Fitz," she said, "you cannot stay here. I like to keep my house neat and tidy. So I don't want a cat. But I will put an ad in the newspaper and find you a good home."

The ad ran in the evening paper:

WANTED:

Good home for fluffy cat named Fitz.

The next day a man and a little girl arrived.

"We've come to see the cat," they said.

"Fine!" said Miss Perkins. "Now, where is that cat?"

She looked all around. "Hmmm . . ." she said. "No Fitz."

"Thank you anyway," said the man and the little girl. And they left.

That night Fitz curled up on
the rug beside Miss Perkins's bed
and began to purr.

"My, that sounds nice," said
Miss Perkins, and she fell asleep.

The next day a woman and a little boy arrived.
"We've come to see the cat," they said.
"Fine!" said Miss Perkins. "Now, where is that cat?"
She looked all around. "Hmmm . . ." she said. "No Fitz."
"Thank you anyway," said the woman and the little boy.
And they left.

That night Fitz licked the tip of Miss Perkins's nose.

"A kiss!" said Miss Perkins. "What a sweet cat you are."

The next day a teenage girl arrived.

"I've come to see the cat," she said.

"Fine!" said Miss Perkins. "Now, where is that cat?"

She looked all around. "Hmmm . . ." she said. "No Fitz."

"Thank you anyway," said the teenage girl. And she left.

That night Fitz slept on top of Miss Perkins's feet.
"My, that feels good," said Miss Perkins.

The next day an old man arrived.

"I've come to see the cat," he said.

"Fine!" said Miss Perkins. "Now, where is that cat?"

She looked all around. "Hmmm . . ." she said. "No Fitz."

"Thank you anyway," said the old man. And he left.

That night Fitz chased a mouse—right out the door.

"A mouse in my house!" cried Miss Perkins. "Oh, Fitz, you are such a clever, brave, *remarkable* cat! How can I ever thank you?"

The next day an old woman arrived.
"I've come to see the cat," she said.
"I'm very sorry," said Miss Perkins,
"but I have decided to keep the cat."
"Thank you anyway," said the old
woman. And she left.

"Did you hear that, Fitz?" called Miss Perkins.
"I have decided to keep you. You are *my* clever,
brave, remarkable cat."

She looked all around.

"Now, where is that cat?"

And Fitz purred, "H O M E !"

The End